Be the Change

Liz Brownlee does readings and workshops, with her assistance dog, Lola, at schools, libraries, literary and nature festivals. She has fun organizing poetry retreats, exhibitions and events, and runs the poetry website Poetry Roundabout. She is a National Poetry Day Ambassador.

Matt Goodfellow is from Manchester. He spends his time writing and touring the UK and beyond visiting schools, libraries and festivals to deliver high-energy, inspirational poetry performances and workshops. Before embarking on his poetry career, Matt spent over 10 years as a primary school teacher. He is a National Poetry Day Ambassador.

Roger Stevens visits schools, libraries and festivals, performing his work and running workshops for young people and teachers. He is a National Poetry Day Ambassador, a founding member of the Able Writers scheme with Brian Moses and runs the award-winning poetry website www. poetry

Other poetry titles from
Macmillan Children's Books

The Same Inside

Reaching the Stars

BE THE CHANGE

POEMS TO HELP YOU SAVE THE WORLD

by
**Liz Brownlee,
Matt Goodfellow
Roger Stevens**

MACMILLAN
CHILDREN'S
BOOKS

For Bob Alderdice and Rob Bostock, educating the
next generation – M. G.

For Emmelie and Jem and all our children's children – L. B.

For the bees. Good luck! – R. S.

First published 2019 by Macmillan Children's Books
an imprint of Pan Macmillan
20 New Wharf Road, London N1 9RR
Associated companies throughout the world
www.panmacmillan.com

ISBN 978-1-5290-1894-3

1 3 5 7 9 8 6 4 2

A CIP catalogue record for this book is available from
the British Library.

Printed and bound by CPI Group (UK) Ltd, Croydon CR0 4YY

Contents

The Natural World

Tricky Questions, Talking Points

Ways to Change the World

Start Now

be the change
you want to see
walk the walk
stand with me

take the challenge
spread the word
we can make
our voices heard

every single
action helps
with a friend
or by yourself

be the change
you want to see
walk the walk
stand with me

Matt Goodfellow

Captain Save-the-Planet

I am Captain Save-the-Planet
I am GREEN
Not green like The Green Lantern
Not green like The Incredible Hulk
No, I am green like the forests
like grass, like ferns
and the green, clean air
that blew across the planet
long ago
I am Captain Save-the-Planet
I am strong
Not strong like my arch enemy Radioactive
   Man
who burns the sky
with invisible rays
Not like Coal Power Man
who spews out deadly fumes
No, I am strong like the wind
turning a million wind turbines
I am strong like the sun
heating a million homes

I am Captain Save-the-Planet
and I am looking for an assistant
Would you care to apply?

Roger Stevens

What would your planet-saving superpower be?

Munch, Crunch,
Packed Lunch . . .

Your packed lunch can
if you plan it
help to save our
ailing planet,
you'll be saving
just by scrapping
straws and packets,
plastic wrapping,
get an eco
box or two
made of wheat straw
or bamboo,
put in your lunch
and with no oil
the shut-tight lid
won't let it spoil,
banish crisps
and juice in boxes,
fill with wraps

and nuts and coxes,
sliced ham rolled up
(roast or parma),
blueberries, grapes
or a banana,
carrot slices
eggs and cheese,
pizza pieces
pickled peas,
naan bread sarnies,
carrot crunch,
sustainable
sustaining lunch!

Liz Brownlee

Packed lunches contribute to a lot of unrecyclable waste products. **You can help!** See how creative you can become making lunches with no plastic packing whatsoever. Have a competition each week to see who has brought the greenest lunch to school! Use a reusable water bottle for drinks. Sometimes a reusable plastic box is the only solution; but these can last a long time.

Couch Superstar

If changing the world seems far-fetched and
  crazy
because, frankly, my dear, you're incredibly
  lazy

more likely to yawn and stretch on the sofa
than strap yourself in to the change
  rollercoaster

here's an idea you mustn't forget:
there are ways you can help without breaking
  a sweat

put on a jumper, keep thermostats low
get a blanket and rug – feel that warm, cosy
  glow

switch electrical equipment off at the wall
now you're part of the change with no effort at
  all

just two tiny things, but look what you are:
a champion of change - a couch superstar

Matt Goodfellow

You can help! Check out the United Nations Sustainable Development Goals website for more tiny things you can do which make a big difference.

Promise

You see them in doorways
you see them in parks
there are so many of them
that after a while
you don't even notice them
We were in Nottingham
and one of them
played a tune on a toy xylophone
and Mum put a five pound note
in his cup
Mum says
as you grow up
you'll find that life doesn't always turn out
as planned
You have to help people
if you can

Roger Stevens

Crisis, a charity for the homeless, says the latest figures
showed that 4,751 people slept rough across England
on any given night in 2017.

Are You Flushed?

Flushing loos will use a quarter
Of your day's amount of water
'If it's yellow, let it mellow'
Science says just let it be
Save the planet, save your wee!

Liz Brownlee

You can help! Yes, it's true – scientists say that it is fine to leave your wee in the loo, and saving water saves energy as well as water, because it has to be pumped through pipes every time you turn on a tap or flush the toilet. You can also save water by turning off the tap in between rinsing your toothbrush.

Richest Boy in the World

Miss Moss divided the class
proportionally
by the wealth in the world
John was one of the hundred multi-billionaires
who owned half
of all the world's money
Six of the class were reasonably well off
The rest of us were the millions
of really poor people
and some of us couldn't even afford a place to live
After the lesson, at playtime, I asked John for a
  crisp
and he gave me the whole packet
and he said,
If I do get rich, when I'm grown up, do you know
  what?
I won't forget you.

Roger Stevens

The richest 1% of the population in the UK own as much as
the poorest 55% of the population.

Funny Fruit and Wonky Veg

make a change
with a simple pledge:
pick funny fruit
and wonky veg

different looks
same great taste
now none of it
need go to waste

Matt Goodfellow

1.3 billion tonnes of food is wasted in the world each year. In a pile it would be roughly the same size as the mountain Ben Nevis. Wonky fruit and veg tastes the same! Does it matter? Food production takes a massive amount of the planet's resources such as oil and water. Disposing of waste also uses energy. **You can help!** Embrace ugly fruit and veg!

Ways I Have Raised Money for Charity This Year

(or attempted to)

Shaved Dad's eyebrows and half his
   moustache off
(in hindsight it would have been better to ask him first and not do it while he was asleep the night before an important business meeting with his new boss)

Dyed my hair pink and wore pyjamas to school
(again, possibly should have checked with the Headteacher, Mrs Jones, that this was OK – she nearly fainted when she saw me)

Did a sponsored run around the school field
   with Stephen
(who had to stop after one lap because the cut grass was playing havoc with his hay fever and he got stung by a wasp)

Made 12 iced fairy cakes to sell at playtime
*(left them on the kitchen worktop where they were
gobbled up by Frankie, the French Bulldog, who
was then violently sick on Mum's fluffy slippers)*

Matt Goodfellow

Please protect your mum's slippers before raising
money for charity.

Recycling Paper

RECYCLING BIN

Each tonne of paper
you recycle here,
saves electric to power
your house for a year

Recycling paper
saves making it new
5 per cent of the power,
and easy to do!

Liz Brownlee

When you recycle, you help reduce pollution, energy, and raw resources such as wood and oil. We are using up to one and a half times as many resources than the planet has to share in a year. As well as recycling paper to save energy, you can buy things second-hand or get things mended instead of buying new.

Grandad's Tomatoes

When you walk into Grandad's greenhouse
you are zapped
by that zingy tomato scent
There they are
tall and green
in their gro bags
with their bright red inviting fruit
You pick some
for the big salad
or for Grandad's favourite
cheese and tomato sandwiches
and you think
I'll just try one
and you have never eaten a tomato as sweet
   before
the sunshine explodes in your mouth
and they are nothing
NOTHING
like the tasteless
cellophane-wrapped tomatoes
you often find in the supermarket

Grandad's tomatoes
last through July, and August, and
     September
and when the very last red ripe tomato is
     eaten
and the last few green tomatoes
are picked for chutney
we are all a little sad
But no one cries
because Grandad saves some seeds
and plants them
and in the spring
brand new tomato plants start to grow
ready for the new summer's
taste sensation

Roger Stevens

Veg and fruit grown at home taste better, contain no
pesticides (unless you put them on!), and are more
sustainable because you only pick what you need.
It also saves on the huge amounts of water used by
commercial growing practices.

Poem for Amina

we need
to believe
in something
right?

believe
in a girl
who turns
water
to light

Matt Goodfellow

Amina Nazarli, from Azerbaijan, invented a device that
generates electric power from raindrops when she was
just 15 years old. Her motto is 'light up one house at a
time.'

My Favourite Thing

*(To the tune of 'My Favourite Things'
from* The Sound of Music, *Rodgers
and Hammerstein.)*

Christmas and birthdays and festive occasions
I gift wrap my gifts in for all celebrations
brown paper packages tied up with string –
sustainable wrap is my favourite thing!

Cream coloured hankies and worn crisp, white
    sheeting,
gathered with ribbons and pretty with
    pleating,
small bells and posies and leaf sprigs for
    trims –
sustainable wrap is my favourite thing!

Red socks, or boxes with green satin sashes,
cards cut in gift tags for fine fancy flashes,
styling recycling to put my gifts in,
sustainable wrap is my favourite thing –

the Christmas season
being the reason
trees are felled is sad,
but then I remember I saved some myself
And so I don't feel soooo bad!

Liz Brownlee

50,000 trees are felled every year just for wrapping paper used in the UK at Christmas. Much wrapping paper is not recyclable, with shiny foil, plastic or glitter. **You can help!** Plain brown paper can be recycled, you can use that with pretty string, which composts quite quickly. Find an original way to wrap presents! Use scraps of colourful fabric or make wrapped gift boxes and reuse them each year.

Glitter Quitter

be a glitter quitter, though it might seem kinda
   drastic
little fish will think it's dinner, when it's really
   microplastic

and the only things we need to glitter
   underneath the waves
are the scales of little fishes that a glitter-
   quitter saves

so be a glitter quitter it's a better thing to be
than a bitter glitter-gluer sending litter to the
   sea

Matt Goodfellow

Glitter on paper remains when the paper has
disintegrated and frees the glitter to the air and water
courses where it travels to the sea. **You can help!** If
you would like to dispose of your glitter safely, wrap it
in something and enclose it inside a container that is
being thrown away.

Things Not to Throw in the Ocean

Cans that once held
fizzy pop
Plastic bottles
and their tops
Plastic knives and forks
and spoons
Plastic bags
Birthday balloons
Anything
made out of rubber
Plastic bags
My little brother*

*Just joking!

Roger Stevens

Balloons and lanterns, even 'eco' ones, that fly into the sky have to come down somewhere on land or sea, becoming litter and harming farm animals and wildlife, particularly turtles and sea birds. They all take years to break down. **You can help!** Switch to bubbles to mark important events!

Ex-specs

fill somebody somewhere
with wide-eyed delight

by giving the gift
of second-hand sight

Matt Goodfellow

The charity Vision Aid says there are around 1.2 billion
people suffering from impaired vision (which untreated
can lead to blindness), because they don't have access
to eye exams and glasses. **You can help!** If you take
your old specs into a participating optician, the charity
will clean, repair and then distribute them to people
who wouldn't otherwise be able to afford them.

A Message to You

Hello, reader
I am very pleased
that you are reading me right now
and I hope you are enjoying me,
and my friends –
all the other poems in this book

But I wonder
did you know that there are
millions of children in the world
who can't read?

They will never see my voice
nor hear my stories
or read my amazing facts
which is such a shame

How hard could it be
I wonder
to begin to change all that?

Roger Stevens

70 million children round the world get no education.
This leads to an inability to earn enough money as an
adult and traps them in poverty; a problem which
carries on with their own children. Extreme poverty
means children may have to work to help support their
family.

Greta Thunberg

When the whole world is deaf
by greed and by choice,
how do you change things
with only your voice?

It's hard to be noticed,
harder to be heard,
but she stood up and spoke,
could not be deterred.

What made them listen?
What cut through their lies?
Not the pollution
or the fast melting ice,

not the experts or science,
not hunger or flood,
not the extinctions,
our hands red with blood,

it was her steady gaze,
on our planet, alight,
her desperate calm,
her demand, make it right,

it's what we'll recall
of her fight for our youth,
her luminous words,
her courage, her truth.

Liz Brownlee

In August 2018, 15-year-old schoolgirl and climate activist Greta Thunberg, from Sweden, started the first school strike for climate to raise awareness for global warming and to call out the people in power who are being indecisive about taking action. She has said: 'Our house is on fire,' but believes that once we start to act, hope is everywhere.

The Greenway

Once there was a highway
It crossed the busy city
It was noisy, it was smelly
It wasn't very pretty
They called it The Distressway
It was chock-a-block with traffic
And all the people of the city
Said it's really tragic
It's noisy and it's noxious
And it's dangerous every day
So they came up with a plan
And built the Greenway

Now the traffic travels
Underground, below the trees
There are parks and paths for walking
There are flowers, there are bees
And mums and dads push pushchairs
Joggers jog and children play
And the traffic flows more freely
Deep down below The Greenway
And everyone agrees that
In the cities of today
Everyone could work together
And build their own

Roger Stevens

The Rose Kennedy Greenway is a mile-and-a-half of
parks in the heart of Boston. The Greenway, a roof
garden atop a highway tunnel, connects people and
the city with beauty and fun.

The First

Tomasz was
the first
to make loom bands
and sell them at breaktime

the first
to dab

the first
to stop dabbing

the first
to floss

the first
to stop flossing

the first
with fidget spinners

the first
to put his hand up
in a lesson about aspirations
when Miss asked who wanted to
change the world for the better

the first
to say he'd do it by inventing something
to stop the glaciers melting
to reverse global warming
to clean up the rivers
and vacuum the sea

but no one can do that, Tomasz,
Miss said, it's impossible

Tomasz smiled
looked her straight in the eye
nothing's impossible, Miss
there's a first time for everything
someone will do it
and I guarantee

I'll
do it first

that person
is me

Matt Goodfellow

It Sucks

they're in the sea
on the shore
playground, park
and café floor

tell the children
in your class:
you don't need them
in your glass!

Spread the message. Shout it! ROAR: let
this be the final
S
T
R
A
W

Matt Goodfellow

Billions of straws are thrown away every year in the UK and they are one of the top ten debris picked up on beaches. They are particularly dangerous to sea birds. Hopefully they will be banned in commercial premises soon. **You can help!** Until the ban, don't use them when out and ban them at home, too – if you must use one, there are lots of reusable straws available to buy which you can carry around with you.

Garden Treasure

Get yourself
a compost bin,
some tiger worms
and put them in,

worms eat waste food
that's stale and old,
and turn it into
garden gold,

the lowly worm
has pooing powers –
to feed your veg
and grow your flowers.

Liz Brownlee

The fewer things that the rubbish men have to collect
from your house, the less energy it takes, saving on
petrol or diesel. If you have a garden, making your own
compost is easy and saves on buying it!

People Are Amazing

I watched this video
of a man in a village
somewhere far away

he had a pile of tyres
in front of him
and a machete
in his hand

a woman came to him
and he measured her foot
against a tyre
and set to work

quietly
quickly
carefully

he sliced away
at the rubber
and measured
pinned
crafted

and he made her some shoes

out of tyres

and I thought

wow

with minds like his

how can we fail?

Matt Goodfellow

Always in My Pocket

You know when you're out and about
and you're in a coffee shop
or eating street food
and you're given plastic cutlery
and you think
that can't be good for the planet
because every day
all that plastic gets thrown away
Well I have come up with
a simple solution
I carry with me
at all times
in my pocket
a real shiny metal spoon

Roger Stevens

The idea for this poem came from a singer songwriter
called Talis Kimberley-Fairbourn who gave everyone in
the audience a spoon at one of her shows specifically
for this purpose. Most of the plastic cutlery used in the
UK and US cannot be recycled.

Feeding the World

One cabbage seedling,
with small stems bowed
and pale leaves furled,

given food and water
and love can grow
a heart to feed the world.

Liz Brownlee

9-year-old Katie Stagliano brought home a tiny
cabbage seedling as part of a school project, and
tended it so well it became an enormous 40lb cabbage!
She donated it to a soup kitchen where it fed 275
people. Katie decided to start vegetable gardens so
that she could donate the produce to help people in
need. Katie's Krops now has 100 gardens across the US,
helping feed hungry people.

It Could Be You

The soon-to-be-saviour of your generation?
You, my friend, and your education.

The person to rescue each struggling nation?
You, my friend, and your education.

The champion of change and new
    innovation?
You, my friend, and your education.

Who lights up the sky with joy and elation?
You, my friend, and your education.

Matt Goodfellow

The Natural World

Congratulations

congratulations
re-forestation
means the people of the world
still get to breathe

congratulations
to all the nations
doing all the work they can
to plant new trees

Matt Goodfellow

Trees are able to remove harmful pollutants from the
air, like carbon, which contribute to climate change,
and are habitats for many plants and animals. Much
vital rainforest has been lost across the world, often
to provide farmland. Recent research finds trees are
our most powerful weapon in the fight against climate
change. **You can help!** Plant a tree – The National
Forest will plant a tree for you if you have no space to
do it yourself.

The Dodo's Lament

passenger pig**E**on
pyrenean ibe**X**
golden **T**oad
western black rh**I**noceros
colombia**N** grebe
steller's sea **C**ow
tasmanian **T**iger

Roger Stevens

Lone Blue Whale

Far out at sea
where wild waves toss
and the wide sky holds
just one albatross,
where light surrounds
and the winds blow long,
there you hear
the lone whale's song,
horizon to horizon
winding on and on.

The air's too weak
to carry the sound
of the pulses and cries
in the water around,
the beat of his heart's song
has oceans to cross,
under a wide sky
and one albatross.
Let him come to no harm
as he dives and he seeks,

breath weeping waterfalls,

cry haunting deeps,

for the lone blue whale

that swims wild and free

has a love song as large

as the wide green sea.

Liz Brownlee

6 out of 13 whale species are endangered. Does this matter? Whales are at the top of the food chain and have an important role in the overall health of the marine environment. Whale (and dolphin) products are used in candles, beauty products like lipstick and perfumes. **You can help!** Use ethically made personal products.

Thank You

Good morning, little bee
It's great to be alive
on this lovely summer's morning
collecting pollen for your hive

Good morning, little bee
I wonder if you knew
So many fruits and foods we eat
depend on bees like you

For as you buzz from flower to flower
You pollinate each one
Without you I'm afraid
The human race would be undone

Good morning, little bee
May I just say this to you
Thank you, little bee
For all the work you do

Roger Stevens

More than 12 factors are causing the decline of bees – including air pollution, pesticides, herbicides, parasites such as the verroa mite and the loss of wildflower habitats. Does this matter? Bees are vital because they fertilize all our food crops. **You can help!** Plant a wildflower patch in your garden, and leave dandelions in the spring as they are an important food source for the first bumble bees.

Cows

The thing about
a herd of cattle,
the front ends moo,
the back ends rattle.

The grass they eat
they then dispense
in numerous clouds
of flatulence –

I've seen the wind
move in the grass,
the more cows eat
the more they pass.

There's cows in poems,
there's cows in art,
but no one says
how much they fart!*

Liz Brownlee

*Now remedied. Cows and sheep produce a lot of methane from their digestive systems. 1kg of beef, produces 30 kg of carbon dioxide and requires 15,000 litres of water. This is why it helps the planet to reduce the amount of meat you eat, as growing vegetables requires much less water and produces much less greenhouse gas. **You can help!** Make more meals a week meat-free.

Help Needed

bluef**I**n tuna

the java**N** rhino

a**D**dax, the screwhorn antelope

saola, the **A**sian unicorn

sumatra**N** tiger

cross river **G**orilla

prz**E**walski's horse

ili pika, the **R**abbit who is magic

Roger Stevens

There are so many endangered animals it can seem very depressing. But lots of people and organizations are trying to help. **You can help!** Did you know that, along with many other animals, you can adopt a Sumatran Tiger?

Jelly Wishes

Nothing pleases turtles
more than a jellyfish,
in fact a see-through jelly's
a favoured snack-time wish.

Floating see-through plastic
looks exactly like a jelly,
but isn't very wholesome
in a little turtle's belly.

He wants a well-filled belly
full of jelly fresh and frilly,
not nasty, ghastly plastic
discarded willy-nilly.

Liz Brownlee

Plastic bags are easily caught by the wind from rubbish
tips and bins. Many are washed into drains, which lead
into rivers, and then the sea, to harm sea creatures.
You can help! Always dispose of bags, and any plastic,
carefully; even better, don't use plastic bags!

Biodiversity

This big old ball of iron and rock
spinning through the galaxy
is home to plants and animals
of great diversity
the giant Ocean Sunfish,
the tiny Red-toothed Shrew
The snub-nosed Sneezing Monkey
Pettong and Booloroo

The Great Spotted Woodpecker
the Lesser Spotted too
So many plants, so many trees
and also me and you
As we journey on I would suggest
with quiet exactitude
we respect our fellow travellers
Not to would just be rude

Roger Stevens

200 creatures become extinct every day.

The Sea Speaks

Get off my bottom!
It's crude and immoral
your big heavy rollers
are smashing up coral.

Get off my bottom!
You hear what I say?
You kill all the fish
then throw most away.

Get off my bottom!
The scars are appalling!
Just get off my bottom –
and stop bottom trawling.

Matt Goodfellow

Bottom trawling destroys the seabed. Huge nets on rollers are weighted down and dragged along the bottom of the sea, smashing and crushing everything. Most of the marine life trapped in the nets is considered 'bycatch' – which is worthless and thrown overboard. **You can help!** Make sure the fish you do eat is MSC certified, sustainably caught.

Orangutan

The forest is the world
to the orangutan,
he seeks no more
than nuts, bark,
insects, fruit and leaves,
they are all he needs,

he has a gentle hold
on his trees.

What does he know
of chocolate, or margarine?
His trees do not make them,

no, only the oil palms
marching like soldiers
to take the trees,

that do not belong
to the orangutan.

Liz Brownlee

Orangutans, one of our closest relatives, are of the most critically endangered creatures on Earth. Their forest is being cut down for palm oil plantations. Palm oil is in almost every manufactured product in the supermarket. **You can help!** Only buy products that contain sustainable palm oil. You can write to manufacturers who use unsustainable palm oil and ask them to switch. You can support initiatives which find other jobs to help people who live by farming palm oil.

Conservation
Conversation

picture a panda
chewing bamboo

where there was one
now there are two

now there are three
now there are four

wait for a while
soon there'll be more

picture a panda
chewing bamboo

reminding us all
what caring can do

Matt Goodfellow

The giant panda is one of the great conservation successes of recent times. The Chinese government has helped to create panda reserves and ensured that large areas of bamboo forests have been protected. Due to this, panda numbers are increasing steadily in the wild.

Food Chains

Please thank all the creatures who
break down the leaves and feed on poo

and then the creatures not so small
that feed on those that creep and crawl

that are the sort that form the kill
of carnivores much bigger still

and then the grazing creatures who
eat grass and drop their fertile poo

and make us thank again those who
remove those piles of poo from view...

for all these creatures need each item
up and down ad infinitum

and if one should become extinct
the others might too, don't you think?

Liz Brownlee

The creatures that make up a food chain form complicated interactions called food webs. In some areas if the food chain is broken by a creature becoming extinct, other animals in that chain might also become extinct. If enough chains are broken this has a devastating effect on a whole habitat. Recent plummeting insect numbers threatens the collapse of all nature. **You can help!** Buy organic if you can. Do not use pesticides or herbicides in your garden. Grow plants that support insects.

Walk in the Woods

Have you ever walked in the woods
maybe with your dog
and enjoyed the dappled shade beneath the
    trees?
And have you ever seen
a patch of ground where there are no trees?
Maybe there are bluebells growing there
And have you ever thought
Do you know what?
That would be a great spot for a factory

Roger Stevens

You can help! Make sure forests and woods everywhere
are felled sustainably by only choosing products and
paper with an FSC certificate.

Snow Leopard

after the mountain was made by rising up

out of the ground, the snow leopard became,

part snow, part snow shadow, part magic,

she lives, hunts, eats in secret realms,

she leaps in the snow, she swims in the snow,

she sleeps tail curled round in the snow,

until twilight seeks her at dawn or dusk

when she rises out of herself,

white shadowed white, breathing white

into the white sky and the white snow

where everything exists by being written in
white.

Liz Brownlee

Bhutan, where some snow leopards live, is a
sustainability success story. Over 70% of Bhutan is
forest and their constitution requires that 60% of
their country must remain forest forever. The country
actually captures and stores twice as much CO_2 as it
emits, and due to its policies it supports populations
of some of the rarest creatures on earth, including the
snow leopard. Their eco-ethical stance also supports
their human population, so if a snow leopard kills a
farm animal, recompense is paid out of the eco-tourism
budget, ensuring the lives of both the snow leopard and
the farmer.

Symbiosis

a coral grouper
and moray eel

work together
to capture a meal

the strangest alliance
under the sea

if they can do it
so can we

Matt Goodfellow

Tricky Questions, Talking Points

Hunger

Let us care, let us share,
let us mobilize,
make sure no baby's meal
is smaller than his eyes.

Liz Brownlee

The United Nations Food and Agriculture Organization estimates that about 815 million people, or 10.7% of the world's population, were suffering from chronic undernourishment in 2016.

Who Owns Planet Earth?

Who owns the Planet Earth?
Who owns the morning?
Who owns the afternoon?
Who owns the day? Who owns the night?

Who owns the stars and moon?
Who owns the ancient forests?
Who owns the mountains high?
Who owns oceans and the shore?

Who owns the bright blue sky?
Who owns the lakes and reservoirs?
Who owns the waterfall?
Who owns the grey clouds full of rain?
Who owns the raindrops as they fall?

Who owns the water in your tap?
Who owns the fishes in the sea?
Who owns the ground we stand on?
Who owns the air we breathe?

Countries and businesses say, We do!
It's well enshrined in law
But are we not stewards of the Earth?
This Earth belongs to all

Roger Stevens

Equality

we gather in peace
all over the world
joining together
each boy and each girl

no need for tear gas
guns or police
all over the world
we gather in peace

sending a message
of what we expect:
equal rights
equal respect

Matt Goodfellow

Women and girls all over the world are still being discriminated against in health, education and the labour market with negative repercussions for their freedom. This results in a gender pay gap. Paying a woman less for doing the same job as a man is also a problem in some countries – although this is illegal in the UK.

Fleeces

Call the fleece police!
this fleece is shedding pieces
and this will never cease
until making fleeces ceases!

Call the fleece police!
Each fleece when washed releases
into our streams and seas
700,000 pieces!

Liz Brownlee

Studies have shown that each time one fleece is
washed 700,000 fibres made of microplastic are shed
into the water. Sea creatures eat them, mistaking them
for food and we eat fish – so end up eating plastic. Any
plastic clothing sheds plastic into the water in each
wash. One way to help is to only buy clothes made of
natural fibres, with fibres that decompose, wool jumpers
for instance. But natural fibres can be more expensive,
and involve unfair labour practices. It's a very tricky
question, this one!

The Bottom Line

We could fish more sensibly
But that's not the bottom line
We could embrace sustainability
But that's not the bottom line
We could use the rainforests wisely
But that's not the bottom line
This is the bottom line
Money, money, money, money, money

Roger Stevens

Crossing the Road

My mate Tommy
(in Year 6, like me)
was waiting to cross the road
and Ali, who is in the infants (Year 1)
was waiting too
so Tommy held his hand
and helped him over
and I didn't think any more of it

But in class
we were talking about countries
how some are developed and rich
how some are poor
and I thought
wouldn't it be great
if the big rich countries
held the small countries' hands
just to help them
over the road

Roger Stevens

Rich countries helping poorer countries towards sustainability and out of poverty-related issues is one of the 17 Sustainable Goals. Apart from being unfair, no one who is hungry and without resources has the ability to think about a sustainable lifestyle. A sustainable world relies on everyone having enough food, water, sanitation, education and access to sustainable jobs.

City

Let's grow bright flowers
on skyscraper towers,

let's make sure the air
is clean everywhere,

let some city streets
be just for our feet,

let all power come
from wind and the sun,

let all traffic be
run on clean energy.

Liz Brownlee

One of the UN's goals is for sustainable cities and
communities. What things would you like to see happen
to make your city more green? Add them to the poem
above. **You can help!** Ask the person driving you to
switch off their engine in standing traffic. This also
saves fuel. Walk, cycle or take a bus when you can.

Toilet Talk

I'm here to talk toilets
which might sound strange
but toilets show all of us
why we must change

I have a toilet
you have one too
but there's 4 million people
without one, who

are living on earth
right now as you read
and all of that sewage
means deadly disease

so I'm here to talk toilets
which might sound strange
but toilets show all of us
why we must change

Matt Goodfellow

Each day, nearly 1,000 children die due to preventable
water and sanitation-related diarrhoeal disease.

It's a Skin Thing

Oi, mate
wouldn't it be great
if loads of fruit and veg and things
had their own
protective skins?

Yeah, wouldn't that
be great . . . ?

Oh, wait . . .

Matt Goodfellow

Buying fruit and vegetables without plastic wrapping
will help to persuade supermarkets to stop using it
unnecessarily.

Getting to the Truth

Some people say
drinking cow's milk is bad
For one thing
cows expel huge volumes
of greenhouse gases
which contribute
to global warming
They say
Drink almond milk.
Almonds are good for you.
And they are.
Very good for you.
But it turns out
that nearly all the world's almonds
are grown in California*
where there are often droughts
And did you know that
in California
it takes
six thousand litres of water

to produce one litre of almond milk?
That's BONKERS!
And farmers are ripping up
healthy citrus groves
to meet the rising demand
for almond milk.

Oatmilk seems to be a better alternative
But the whole point is this.
Don't always accept
what you read on a label.
Or what people tell you.
Don't always believe what you read
in the papers
or see on TV
or on the internet
If you really want to help
Just dig a little deeper
Try and get to the truth

Roger Stevens

*around 80%

Windmills on My Mind

(Based on the song 'The Windmills of Your Mind' written by Alan and Marilyn Bergman.)

Like a circle in a spiral
like a planet out in space
a windmill keeps on turning
with the wind upon its face
like a watch that needs no winding
as it's spinning hour by hour
it turns and turns a turbine
to make electric power

without producing gases
using just the wind and breeze
no radioactive danger
and without polluting seas

to save Earth and mankind
the energy dream I find
is the windmills in my mind

the trouble is that people
don't like how they appear
and protest very hotly
I don't want those windmills here
so the world it keeps on burning
with our lives all on the line
I know I'd choose the windmills
if the choosing was all mine

without producing gases
using just the wind and breeze
no radioactive danger
and without polluting seas

to save Earth and mankind
the energy dream I find
is the windmills in my mind

Liz Brownlee

Is it better to have windmills in our hills and save the
planet, or save a view?

No Joke

How many planets
can you save by changing
a lightbulb?

One.

Matt Goodfellow

Replacing halogen light bulbs with LEDs can reduce the
electricity used by 90% and save hundreds of pounds
a year. **You can help!** Switch off lights as you leave a
room!

Weathering Weather

Where green grass dies
and wind blows dry
while ground grows cracks
and sun burns high,

where all the thirsty
call in pain
hoping, praying
rain falls again,

where more tornadoes
whirl around,
or piles of snow
engulf the ground,

where rain pours down
and drainpipes gush
and banks are breached
as rivers rush,

where sea floods fields
where crops are grown,
drowning cattle
and people's homes,

where temperatures
are out of range,
you're weathering weather,
that's climate change.

Liz Brownlee

The warming climate, climate change, will mean more
extreme weather in many parts of the world. The worst
hit will be low-lying countries and the poorest countries,
who find it hardest to prepare and recover.

Listening Bench

If you're new to the school
or speak a different language
sit yourself down
on the Listening Bench
One of our team
of Year 6* interpreters
will come
and talk to you
and listen to you
so that you don't feel lonely
We think it's such a great thing
that we are writing
to the Prime Minister about it
so that every school
in the country
will have a Listening Bench
Maybe every village and town
could have one too
so that lonely people
who speak a different language

and immigrants from war-torn countries
wouldn't feel alone
and would have someone to talk to
someone who will listen

*And Jasmine, who is in Year 5 but brilliant
   at languages.

                                        Roger Stevens

A Polar Plea

I'd really like you humans
to take your own advice
as the planet's getting warmer
polar bears are paying the price
the glaciers are melting
and we're going to capsize
I'm starving for some blubber
and I cannot ask you twice
for my feet are getting wetter
as I'm standing on thin ice.

Liz Brownlee

Polar bears are already feeling the effects of ice melting. The oceans of the world absorb a lot of the heat and the CO_2 we send into the atmosphere. This has many effects, including warming of the oceans, and making them more acidic. Acid seas affect many ocean creatures including coral. **You can help!** All life on Earth is connected to the ocean. Any steps you take to reduce the energy you use will help the ocean. Can you think of any other ways to help?

Dump It

Dump that mattress
I don't care
in the woodland
over there
Plastic trimmings
unwanted card
a bag of concrete
from the yard
Dad's done the drive
and dumped some gravel
he says the tip's
too far to travel
Our old computer
and TV
The mess?
It doesn't worry me
So what? They say
it's a disgrace
Just don't dump it
near *our* place

Roger Stevens

Let Us Save the Planet

Let us save the planet
One step at a time
One paper bag at a time
One re-useable water bottle at a time
One light switched off at a time
One encouraging word at a time
One vegetarian option at a time
One cycle ride at a time
One moment of compassion at a time
One chat to the old person on the bus at a
    time
One cheery word to a homeless person at a
    time
One windmill at a time
One free range organic egg at a time
One poster at a time
One planted seed at a time
One good deed at a time
One hug at a time
One poem at a time

And over time
All those one at a times
Will help save the planet

Roger Stevens

Snow

As they swirl
in lilting flight,
as cold as stars,
in soundless white,

their drifting feathers
spread their wings,
and sing the songs
that snowflakes sing,

of how small gifts
of peace and light
can change the world
in just one night.

Liz Brownlee